NDERKIDZ

e Berenstain Bears®: Kindness Counts
pyright © 2010 by Berenstain Bears, Inc.
strations © 2010 by Berenstain Bears, Inc.

quests for information should be addressed to:
nderkidz, *Grand Rapids, Michigan* 49530

rary of Congress Cataloging-in-Publication Data

enstain, Jan, 1923-
   The Berenstain Bears : kindness counts / by Jan and Mike Berenstain.
        p. cm.
   Summary: Brother Bear's act of kindness is repaid when he share his knowledge of airplane
delmaking with young Billy. Includes Bible verses.
   ISBN 978-0-310-71257-2 (softcover)
   [1. Airplanes—Models—Fiction. 2. Kindness—Fiction. 3. Conduct of life—Fiction. 4. Christian life—
tion. 5. Bears—Fiction.] I. Berenstain, Michael. II. Title. III. Title: Kindness counts.
   PZ7.B44826Bh 2011
   [E]—dc22   2009022674

tor: *Mary Hassinger*
   direction: Cindy Davis

ted in China

11 12 13 14 15 /LPC/ 27 26 25 24 23 22 21 20 19 18 17 16 15 14 13 12 11 10 9 8 7 6 5 4 3 2 1

The Berenstain Bears®
Kindness Counts

written by Jan and Mike Berenstain

ZONDERVAN.com/
AUTHORTRACKER
follow your favorite authors

ZONDERk‘dz

Living Lights™

Brother Bear was a bear of many interests. He enjoyed sports such as baseball, soccer, football, and basketball. He liked to draw and paint, and he was interested in science. He had hobbies like collecting stamps and baseball cards, and he enjoyed fishing and playing video games. But the thing he enjoyed most of all was building model airplanes.

He started building models with Papa when he was very young. At first, they made simple plastic models. But, soon, they were creating flying models out of lightweight wood and paper. Before long, Brother could build models all by himself.

He kept building bigger and better models that could fly longer, farther, and higher. On trips to the park with Sister Bear, he always took along his latest model for flight trials. It was a thrill to wind its propeller for the first time, let it go, and watch it fly across the park.

One Saturday afternoon, Brother tried out his latest creation, a big model plane painted bright red called *The Meteor*. He set it down on the grass and wound the propeller. Sister joined some of her friends nearby. One of them was minding her younger brother, Billy. He was playing with a small model plane like the ones Brother had when he was little.

When Billy saw Brother's big new plane, he came over to take a look.

"Wow!" he said. "That's beautiful!"

"Thanks! She's called *The Meteor*. I built her myself," Brother said proudly.

"Wow!" said Billy. "I wish I could build a plane like that."

Brother finished winding the propeller and picked up *The Meteor*.
"Can I help you fly it?" asked Billy.

Brother was proud of his models and careful with them too. They took a long time to build and were easy to break. If you didn't launch them just right, they could take a nosedive and crash.

"Well," said Brother doubtfully, "I don't know…," But he remembered how Papa always let him help out when they were building and flying model planes. That's how he learned—by helping Papa.

"Well," said Brother, "okay. You can help me hold it."

"Oh, boy! Thanks!" said Billy.

Brother knelt down and let Billy hold the model with him.

"Now, remember," said Brother, "don't throw it—let it fly out of your hands. Here we go— one, two, three ... *fly!*"

They both let go, and the big red *Meteor* lifted up and away, its propeller whirring.

"YIPEEE!" yelled Billy. "Look at it fly!"

But Brother was worried. *The Meteor* was climbing up too steeply. As they watched, *The Meteor* rose high above the park. It seemed to pause in midair. Its nose suddenly dipped down, and it went into a dive. *The Meteor* hit the ground with a nasty *crunch*!

Brother and Billy ran to the wrecked model. Brother sadly picked it up and looked at the damage. Billy's big sister and the others noticed the excitement and came over.

"Oh, no!" said Billy. "Is it my fault? Did I do something wrong? Did I throw it instead of letting it fly like you said?"

Brother shook his head. "Of course not!" he said. "You did fine. This is my fault. I didn't get the balance right. It's tail heavy. That's why it went up too steep, paused, and dove down. That's called 'stalling.'"

"Are you going to fix it?" asked Billy.

"Sure!" laughed Brother. "'Build 'em, fly 'em, crash 'em, fix 'em!' That's my motto."

"Could I help you?" wondered Billy.

"Now, Billy," said his big sister, "you're too young to help."

But Brother remembered how Papa always used to let him help. That was how he learned about model airplanes.

"That's okay," Brother told Billy's big sister. "I don't mind. I could use a little help."

So Billy came along to the Bears' tree house. Mama and Papa were pleased that Brother was being so kind to young Billy.

"It's just as the Good Book says," Mama said, "'Blessed are the merciful, for they will be shown mercy.'"

"Yes," agreed Papa, "and it also says in the Bible that a kind person benefits himself."

"What does that mean?" wondered Brother.

"It means that no act of kindness is wasted," said Papa. "Any kindness you do will always come back to you."

Blessed are
the merciful,
for they will
be shown
mercy.
Matthew 5:7

Every afternoon that week, Billy helped Brother work on the plane. He didn't know very much, but he learned a lot and he had lots of fun. Brother had fun too. He enjoyed teaching, and he liked having a helper who looked up to him.

The next Saturday, *The Meteor* was ready for another flight. Brother and Billy took it down to the park. Everyone came along to watch. They wound *The Meteor's* propeller, held it up, and let it fly. It lifted away and rose in a long, even curve.

"This looks like a good flight!" said Brother.

The Meteor flew on and on across the field. Slowly, it came down, landing clear on the other side of the park in a three-point landing. Brother and Billy ran over. It was in perfect shape.

"Hurray!" yelled Billy, jumping up and down.

Brother began to wind up the propeller for another try, but he noticed a group of older cubs coming into the park. They carried a lot of interesting equipment and wore jackets that said "Bear Country Rocket Club." Brother went over to watch. They were setting up a model rocket. They were going to fire it off and let it come down by parachute. Brother was excited.

"Excuse me," he said to the cub in charge, "do you think I could help you launch the rocket?"

The cub shook his head. "Sorry!" he said. "You're too young. It's too dangerous."

Brother walked away sadly. But he noticed that Billy was staying behind. He was talking to the older cub in charge. The older cub called Brother back.

"My cousin, Billy, tells me you let him help with your model plane," said the older cub. Brother just nodded. The older cub smiled. "That was cool. You seem to know a lot about flying and models. I guess you can help out."

So the rocket club let Brother hold things for them, carry things for them, and squirt a little glue here and there. He learned a lot and he was happy. When it was time to fire off the rocket, they even let Brother push the button.

"10, 9, 8, 7, 6, 5, 4, 3, 2, 1 ... *fire!*" said the cub in charge, and Brother pushed the button.

There was a loud *WHOOOSH*!

The rocket shot up, leaving a trail of smoke.

High above the park a yellow parachute popped open, and the rocket drifted back to earth.

They ran over to it. It was all twisted and scorched.

"Are you going to fix it?" asked Brother.

"Sure," laughed the older cub. "'Build 'em, fly 'em, crash 'em, fix 'em!' That's our motto."

"Could I help you?" asked Brother.

The older cub thought it over. "Sure," he said, slapping Brother on the back. "Why not?"

So, because Brother Bear had shown a little kindness to someone younger than himself, he became the youngest member, ever, of the Bear Country Rocket Club.

And was he ever proud!